Welcome to ALADDIN QUIX!

If you are looking for fast, fun-to-read stories
with

endly
humo... ...ing
story... ...n
ALADDIN QUIX is for you!

But wait, there's more!

If you're also looking for stories with
tables of contents; word lists; about-the-
book questions; 64, 80, or 96 pages; short
chapters; short paragraphs; and large fonts,
then **ALADDIN QUIX** is *definitely* for you!

ALADDIN QUIX: The next step between ready
to reads and longer, more challenging chapter
books, for readers five to eight years old.

Read more ALADDIN QUIX books!

By Stephanie Calmenson

Our Principal Is a Frog!
Our Principal Is a Wolf!
Our Principal's in His Underwear!
Our Principal Breaks a Spell!
Our Principal's Wacky Wishes!

Royal Sweets
By Helen Perelman

Book 1: *A Royal Rescue*
Book 2: *Sugar Secrets*
Book 3: *Stolen Jewels*
Book 4: *The Marshmallow Ghost*
Book 5: *Chocolate Challenge*

A Miss Mallard Mystery
By Robert Quackenbush

Dig to Disaster
Texas Trail to Calamity
Express Train to Trouble
Stairway to Doom
Bicycle to Treachery
Gondola to Danger
Surfboard to Peril
Taxi to Intrigue

Little Goddess Girls
By Joan Holub and Suzanne Williams

Book 1: *Athena & the Magic Land*
Book 2: *Persephone & the Giant Flowers*
Book 3: *Aphrodite & the Gold Apple*
Book 4: *Artemis & the Awesome Animals*
Book 5: *Athena & the Island Enchantress*
Book 6: *Persephone & the Evil King*
Book 7: *Aphrodite & the Magical Box*
Book 8: *Artemis & the Wishing Kitten*

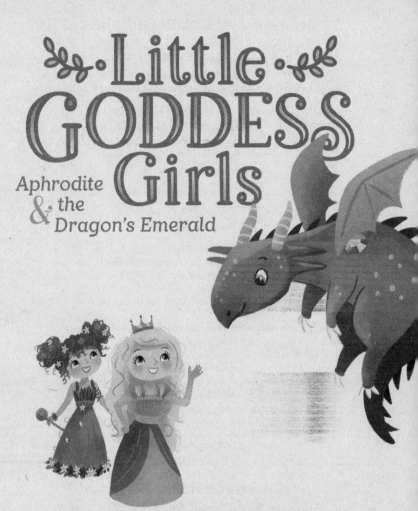

Little GODDESS Girls

Aphrodite & the Dragon's Emerald

JOAN HOLUB & SUZANNE WILLIAMS

ALADDIN QUIX

New York   London   Toronto   Sydney   New Delhi

ALADDIN QUIX

Simon & Schuster Children's Publishing Division

1230 Avenue of the Americas, New York, New York 10020

First Aladdin QUIX paperback edition May 2023

Text copyright © 2023 by Joan Holub and Suzanne Williams

Illustrations copyright © 2023 by Yuyi Chen

Also available in an Aladdin QUIX hardcover edition.

All rights reserved, including the right of reproduction in whole or in part in any form.

ALADDIN and the related marks and colophon are registered trademarks of Simon & Schuster, Inc.

For information about special discounts for bulk purchases, please contact Simon & Schuster Special Sales at 1-866-506-1949 or business@simonandschuster.com.

The Simon & Schuster Speakers Bureau can bring authors to your live event. For more information or to book an event contact the Simon & Schuster Speakers Bureau at 1-866-248-3049 or visit our website at www.simonspeakers.com.

Designed by Tiara Iandiorio

The illustrations for this book were rendered digitally.

The text of this book was set in Archer Medium.

Manufactured in the United States of America 0323 OFF

2 4 6 8 10 9 7 5 3 1

This book has been cataloged with the Library of Congress.

ISBN 978-1-6659-0411-7 (hc)

ISBN 978-1-6659-0410-0 (pbk)

ISBN 978-1-6659-0412-4 (ebook)

Cast of Characters

Aphrodite (af•row•DIE•tee): Golden-haired goddess girl who has a small crown, a golden apple, and a chariot drawn by doves

Persephone (purr•SEFF•uh•nee): Goddess girl with flowers and clovers growing in her hair and clothes, who has a magic cane

Cut-Ups (CUT•upps): Paper people that can walk and talk

Athena (uh•THEE•nuh): Brown-haired goddess girl with winged sandals

Artemis (AR•tuh•miss):
Black-haired goddess girl with a bow
and arrow, and a heart necklace

Hestia (HESS•tee•uh): Small,
winged Greek goddess who helps
four goddess-girl friends

Zeus (ZOOSS): Most powerful of the
Greek gods, who lives in Sparkle City
and can grant wishes

Pygmalion (pig•MAYL•yun): A
prince who creates paper people

Galatea (GAL•uh•TEE•uh):
Pygmalion's paper girlfriend

Medusa (muh•DOO•suh): Mean
mortal girl with snakes for hair, whose
stare turns other mortals to stone

Contents

1

Missing Jewels

Aphrodite straightened the small, shiny crown she wore. She flipped her long golden hair out of her eyes and looked back over her shoulder.

"Come on, **Persephone**!" she

called, waving at her friend to catch up.

Persephone had stopped way behind her on the Hello Brick Road. It led to places all over **Mount Olympus**—this magical land where the two girls lived. Today they hoped the road would lead them to a treasure. A stolen **emerald**!

Aphrodite pointed ahead to a tall castle. Flags flew high atop its four corner towers. "**Hurry!** I see the Kingdom of **Cut-Ups**," she called. The Kingdom's castle was where they hoped to find the emerald.

"Coming! First I want to help these flowers!" Persephone called back. She was standing next to some droopy daisies growing alongside the road.

Not long ago, Persephone had been given the gift of good luck. This had boosted a magical skill she'd always had—growing plants. In fact, real leaves and flowers grew on her dress and in her curly red hair!

Aphrodite watched Persephone

wave her hand across the patch of sad daisies. *Zing!* Like magic, the flowers brightened and smiled.

They and their other two best friends, **Athena** and **Artemis**, were **goddess** girls. A tiny, winged grown-up goddess named **Hestia** had told them so!

Hestia had also said that they all had special, magical powers. Persephone could help things grow. Athena was super-duper smart. And Artemis could talk to animals.

If only I knew what my magical

power was, thought Aphrodite.

She did have a magic apple and a magic chariot. But that wasn't the same as having her own magical *power*.

While Aphrodite waited for Persephone to catch up, she played her hopping game. The Hello Brick Road was made of orange, blue, and pink bricks. She hopped from one pink brick to the next.

Just minutes ago, she and Persephone had left the Castle of What-Ifs. They'd gone there looking for a stolen **ruby**. Cute, talking bunnies called the What-Ifs lived there. Those bunnies had worried about very silly things. One of them had worried that a bald giant would steal the bunny king's ears to make a furry hat!

The two girls *had* found the ruby there. Now it was tucked safely in Persephone's pocket.

Behind her, Aphrodite heard the daisies speak to Persephone. **"Thank you!"** they sing-songed. "Will you stay and play with us? Please, please, *please*?"

Aphrodite stopped hopping and looked back. Persephone had begun poking holes around the flowers with her magic silver cane. Hestia had given her the cane during one of their many fun adventures. Her pokes would probably help those flowers grow even taller.

Before Persephone could answer the daisies, Aphrodite ran back and grabbed her hand. "I'm very sorry, but my friend can't play today. Gotta go!" Aphrodite told the daisies. Then she hurried Persephone off toward the Kingdom of Cut-Ups.

Persephone waved back at the flowers. "Bye! Nice to meet you! Have fun growing!"

"I wonder if Athena or Artemis have found any **jewels** yet," Aphrodite said as they rushed on. It was only yesterday that a ruby, an emerald, a **pearl**, and a **diamond** had all gone missing from Sparkle City. Without them, the city had become foggy and gloomy.

If those jewels weren't returned by tonight, **Zeus** wouldn't be able to protect the city if trouble came. He was just an eight-year-old boy—the same age as Aphrodite and her friends. Yet he was the super-duper powerful king of all the Greek **gods**! He could throw *real* thunderbolts! And he ruled Sparkle City, high atop Mount Olympus.

Aphrodite and her friends had quickly found out who had stolen the jewels: the Four-Winds! The East Wind had blown the ruby to the Castle of What-Ifs. The South Wind had whisked the emerald to the Kingdom of Cut-Ups. Persephone and Aphrodite had come looking for it.

Meanwhile Athena had gone north to hunt for the missing pearl.

It had been whirled away
by the North Wind. And
Artemis had gone west,
since the West Wind had
huff-puffed the diamond
there.

"Hey, that castle
is staring at us,"
Persephone said,
pointing ahead.

"Huh?"
Aphrodite
looked

to see what Persephone meant. **Whoa!** Big stone faces as tall as them *were* watching them from the walls. As the girls hurried toward the faces, they heard a flapping sound overhead. They looked up.

Something big and purple was flying above them. It had wings, claws, and a beak like a bird. But no feathers. Suddenly it dove, zooming right at them!

"It's a . . . a purple people-eater!" shouted Aphrodite. "Run!"

2

Paper People

Aphrodite and Persephone raced for the castle. The big purple flying thing zoomed after them.

As they ran, Persephone touched the four-leaf clovers that grew in her hair. Aphrodite hoped their good-luck magic was working. Because it would be very *bad* luck if the girls got clawed by that purple thing. Or worse—eaten!

"It's coming closer!" shouted Persephone.

"Watch out!" Aphrodite yelled as the thing swooped toward them.

Swoosh! Whoosh! The girls ducked, but not fast enough. The purple thing pecked the top of Aphrodite's head. "Ow!" she said.

From up close, she could see it

wasn't a purple people-eater after all. It was a dragon!

"That wacky dragon just stole my twinkly thinking crown!" Aphrodite wailed. She shook her fist at it. The crown had been a gift from Zeus. It wasn't just pretty. It helped her remember to think before she said things that might hurt others' feelings. Without it, she probably wouldn't have remembered to speak kindly to those daisies earlier.

The dragon was flying high again, now wearing *her* crown!

"It's coming back!" she called to Persephone. "Use your silver cane to knock my crown off its head!"

"What? My silver cane?" Persephone stopped and looked around in surprise. "It's gone!"

Swoosh! The dragon swooped again, grinning big. Not only was it wearing Aphrodite's crown, it was also holding Persephone's cane in its teeth!

"Give back my cane!" yelled Persephone, waving her arms.

"Yeah, and give me my crown, too!" yelled Aphrodite.

A blast of wind shot at them from the dragon's nose. It was hot and smelly. *Ewww!* The girls covered their faces and ran the rest of the way to the castle. There they pushed through the front doors without even knocking. Finally they were safe inside, where that creature couldn't get them!

Before they could shut the doors behind them, however, voices inside the castle began to yelp. "**Oh *nooo!* Help!** When the wind starts to blow, up we go!"

Aphrodite and Persephone turned to see dozens and dozens of large pieces of paper. They were floating high in the air around the girls. Many had pictures or words on them. Some had been cut into shapes, like hearts or rectangles.

"Shut those doors!" the papers shouted at them. "You're letting the wind in!"

The dragon's breath had whooshed in through the huge open doors, Aphrodite realized. And it was making these papers whirl and twirl!

Thunk! Thunk! She and Persephone quickly pushed the castle doors shut.

Right away the wind stopped. The papers began to float back down. Upon touching the ground, each one stood up. *Stood up?* Yes! Because it turned out that each piece of paper had legs. And arms and a head, too!

"What *are* you?" Aphrodite asked as the last of the papers drifted down.

"Kites?" Persephone guessed.

"No! We are paper people," a frowny-faced rectangle answered. Like many of the papers, it stood as tall as the two girls.

"I'm a school report card!" the rectangle told them. "And I give

your arrival here a grade A for Awful. I also give you a B for Bad manners, a C for Causing trouble, a D for Destruction, and an F for Failing to knock on the door before entering our kingdom!"

The girls didn't have time to reply, because just then, a pink birthday card ran over to them. There was a picture of a cake on its front.

"Happy birthday!" it called happily.

"Thank you, but it's not my birthday," Persephone told it.

"Mine either," said Aphrodite.

"Doesn't matter! I just wanted to cheer you up after you got bad grades!" The card smiled at them and then cartwheeled away.

"Thanks. That was nice of you!" Persephone called after it.

Aphrodite looked around at all the papers. "So you're really *people*? Made of *paper*?" she asked.

"Yes, and we just *love* visitors," said a red paper heart.

"Welcome!" boomed a bunch of voices all at once. They came from the castle wall itself. Those big stone faces she'd seen on the outside of the castle had turned to face the inside now. And they were speaking!

"A castle with talking walls and paper people? That's so weird!" Aphrodite said in surprise.

The wall faces and the papers all frowned at her. They didn't look welcoming at all anymore. "Our castle isn't weird! How dare you!" they grumped.

Oops! Without her crown, Aphrodite had forgotten to think before speaking. She'd hurt their feelings.

Suddenly she sneezed.

Ah-choo! "Um, s-s-sorry. Paper dust. It makes me sneeze." She sneezed again. So did Persephone. With each sneezy breeze, paper people tumbled over and flew up in the air again.

Stomp! Stomp! Stomp! Stomp! Four paper soldiers came marching down from the castle towers. "Sneezing is against the rules of our kingdom!" they shouted at Aphrodite and Persephone.

3

Pygmalion

Each of the four marching soldiers carried a flagpole from one of the castle towers. On the end of each pole waved a colorful paper flag. The soldiers poked the tips of their poles toward the two girls.

"We're taking you to Prince **Pygmalion**," a red paper soldier told them.

"Who's Pygmalion?" Aphrodite and Persephone asked at the same time.

"The boss of the Kingdom of Cut-Ups, that's who!" said a blue soldier.

"We do whatever he says," said a pink soldier. "We owe him big-time because he can make all of us paper people come alive!"

"And also because he has big,

sharp scissors!" added a purple soldier.

Uh-oh! thought Aphrodite. That sounds dangerous. "But we did not know there was a no-sneezing rule!" she told them.

A paper sign standing nearby pointed at itself. "What? But the rule is written right here on me!"

"No, it isn't!" Persephone said. "You're blank."

The sign looked down at itself. "Oh, sorry." It turned around. Now they could see the warnings printed on its back:

NO SNEEZES! NO BREEZES! NO WHEEZES. OR ELSE!

"No fair!" huffed Aphrodite. "We didn't see those warnings."

"Right! So you really can't

blame us," added Persephone.

The soldiers poked the tips of their flagpoles toward the girls again. "Rules are rules. Now move it!"

Having no choice, the girls went in the direction the soldiers pushed them. The other paper people stayed behind. Soon they all reached a tall, round tower in the middle of the castle.

The soldiers marched the girls inside and up its winding stone staircase. It led them to a big, fancy room at the top of the tower. There were pretty paper curtains on its windows and colorful paper flowers in pots set all around.

Everywhere they looked, they saw shelves of paper. Some of it was rolled up. Most sat in crooked stacks. Paper hearts were scattered all over the stone floor.

Across the room, a boy wearing a crown sat working at a long table. His back was toward them. There were paints, pencils, and more

large pieces of paper on his table. **Snip! Snip!** went his big scissors. He was cutting paper into big shapes! One was in the shape of a ballerina. He painted a face on it. When he set it on the floor, it smiled, twirled, and then danced off down the tower stairs.

The soldiers pushed Aphrodite and Persephone toward the table. The boy stopped cutting and turned around. His eyes got big with surprise when he saw them.

"Who are these girls?" he asked

the soldiers. "Why did you bring them here?"

The blue soldier pointed at Aphrodite and Persephone. "Because they sneezed, Prince Pygmalion!" he explained.

Pygmalion frowned at the girls. "Sneezing is against the rules in the Kingdom of Cut-Ups! You see, paper is light and thin. So even a gentle breeze can blow my paper people around. It could scatter them far outside the castle walls until they're lost forever!"

"We didn't know!" said Aphrodite.

The prince turned on his stool and then leaped to stand. "That's no excuse! I built this kingdom to keep out our enemy, the South Wind. We don't need trouble-makers like you here."

"Let's punish them!" all four soldiers yelled at once.

Roar! A paper lion cutout jumped up from the prince's table. "I could bite them," it offered.

"Or I could scare them," sug-

gested a paper witch. It lifted off
the table and began circling the
room on its flying broom.

"Let me kick them!" said
a paper ninja. It leaped
from the table and did
an air kick, yelling,
"Kee-YAH!"

Aphrodite didn't
think paper

people could bite or kick very hard. And they weren't very scary, either. Before she could say so, the paper witch flew out a window. And the lion and ninja jumped out of it to float downstairs.

Then Persephone spoke up. "Please!" she begged. "We don't have time for this. We're here to find a green emerald. Can you help us?"

"Yeah! If you have it, you'd better give it to us. Right now!" Aphrodite demanded. Persephone poked her in the side with her elbow.

"Ow!" Aphrodite cried out. She sent Persephone a hurt look.

"Sorry, but yelling like that is no way to get this prince to help us," her friend whispered.

"Oh, you're probably right," Aphrodite whispered back. She turned to Pygmalion. "I lost my twinkly thinking crown. Without it, I sometimes forget to think before I speak—er, yell. What I meant to say was . . . *please* help us find the emerald."

Pygmalion stared at the girls

as he raised his scissors. **Snip!**
Snip!

Uh-oh! Is he thinking about snip-
ping us? wondered Aphrodite.
The girls each took a step back.
Luckily, he only began to cut out
more paper hearts.

"Zeus needs that emerald to help
protect Sparkle City," Persephone
explained. "Without it, the city has
turned foggy and gloomy."

"We think the emerald is some-
where in this castle," Aphrodite
went on. "We need to take it to

Thunderbolt Tower along with three other jewels. Only then will Sparkle City **sparkle** again."

"Why can't Zeus just fix the city with his magic powers?" Pygmalion asked.

Because he's still learning how to use those powers, Aphrodite thought, but didn't say out loud. Because Zeus had warned the goddess girls not to tell anyone. If his enemies found out he wasn't all-powerful, they might try to attack his city!

Aphrodite rushed to change the subject. Looking around the room, she asked the prince, "Do you make all the paper people that live in this kingdom?"

At her question, Pygmalion brightened and seemed to forget about Zeus. "Yes, I cut them out of paper, then paint them," he said.

"Doesn't that hurt them? When you cut the paper, I mean?" Persephone asked.

Pygmalion shook his head. "No, they don't come alive until I give them faces. I paint those on last of all. Watch." He set his scissors on his worktable and picked up an unpainted paper scarecrow. Quickly he painted a face on it.

The scarecrow's eyes blinked open. Then its mouth grinned. **"Woo-hoo!"** it shouted. "I'm off to shoo paper crows away from the paper veggies growing in the castle garden." It jumped from the table and ran downstairs.

Pygmalion smiled. "Creating paper cut-ups makes me happy.

Only for a little while, though." He sighed and looked toward a corner of the room, where a white cloth sheet hung. "Now I'm sad again. Too sad for more talk."

Suddenly he turned to his soldiers. "Take these girls away and lock them up!" he ordered.

With that, he turned his back on Aphrodite and Persephone and began cutting out more hearts. The soldiers came closer, circling the girls. *Uh-oh!*

4

Girlfriend

"Wait! Tell us why you're sad," Persephone begged Pygmalion. "Maybe we can help. Right?" She elbowed Aphrodite in the side again.

"Ow! Uh, right," Aphrodite

agreed. If they could make Pygmalion happy again, he might not punish them. Too bad he didn't pay their suggestion any attention, though.

Meanwhile the soldiers moved closer.

Just then, a large book sitting beside a stack of papers jumped off a shelf. It rushed up to the two girls before the soldiers could. There was a lock on its front cover with a key in it.

"Psst, I'm Pygmalion's diary,"

the book whispered to the girls. "Want to know why he's sad?"

"Yes! Why?" Aphrodite whispered back. She and Persephone leaned closer to the diary, so the prince wouldn't hear.

"Sorry, I can't tell you. Diaries are secret," said the diary. "But you can make guesses."

"Okay—" Persephone started to say.

But the diary cut her off. Suddenly its key popped out of its lock. The diary burst open. Its pages were filled with writing and small drawings Pygmalion must have made. On one page, he'd drawn a heart around the letters P + G.

"**Oh!** I have so many secrets. I can't help myself. **I just have to tell!**" yelled the diary. "The reason Pygmalion has been making lots of heart shapes lately is because he's in love!"

Hearing this, the prince leaped up. "Blabbermouth!"

Pygmalion ran over to them, pushing his soldiers aside. He grabbed his diary, shut it, and locked it. After setting it back on its shelf, he turned to the girls and spread his arms wide. **It's true!** I *am* in love!"

Then he slumped. "But my love is hopeless." He went over and brushed some newly made heart-shaped paper people off his worktable. They began twirling around the room.

"How do you do it? Make your paper come alive, I mean," Aphrodite asked him.

Pygmalion shrugged. "I've always been good at making cut-outs. One day, a goddess named Hestia visited here and admired them. She gave me the magic touch to bring them to life."

"Hestia?" Persephone and Aphrodite both said in surprise.

"We know her too," said

Aphrodite. "She told us we're goddess girls."

"You're goddesses?" Pygmalion jumped off his stool. "What kind of magic can you do?"

"Mostly spells. We're still pretty new at magic," said Persephone.

Pygmalion came closer. "If you use your goddess powers to help me, I'll help you find that emerald you're looking for. And no punishment for sneezing. Deal?"

Quickly the girls nodded. What else could they do?

Grinning now, the prince ran over to a corner of the room. **Whoosh!** There he pushed aside the white cloth sheet he'd been staring at earlier. A girl stood behind it. A green paper girl as tall as Aphrodite!

She and Persephone gasped when they saw it. The green girl wore a frown. And there were curly paper snakes on top of her head instead of hair!

Pygmalion waved his hand toward the paper girl, a proud

smile on his face. "Meet my girl-friend! I made her and named her Princess **Galatea**."

Aphrodite and Persephone backed away, staring at the paper girl in shock. Because she looked exactly like a real girl they

knew. And she was *not* a nice girl.

"I've tried to bring Galatea to life, but it didn't work. Maybe you could?" Pygmalion begged.

"*No!*" Aphrodite and Persephone shouted together.

He crossed his arms, looking angry. "Why not?"

"Because Galatea looks exactly like this evil girl we know. Her name's **Medusa**," Aphrodite told him.

"Last time we saw her, she got turned into a stone **statue** in a forest," added Persephone.

Pygmalion nodded, excited. "Yes! I saw that statue when I went on a walk around Mount Olympus. When I came back, I created Galatea to look just like it."

"Hmm. I wonder if maybe that Medusa statue somehow put a spell on you? A spell to make you create Galatea with Medusa's same powers," Aphrodite said to Pygmalion. "So she'd make trouble and do evil stuff around here."

"Yeah! Before she became a

statue, Medusa could turn living creatures to stone. With a single **zap** from her eyes!" Persephone said. "So if we wake up Galatea, there's a chance she might zap *you*."

The prince only smiled wider at his paper girlfriend. "I'm sure Galatea wouldn't do that. She looks super nice. And *sooo* beautiful!" He put both hands over his heart and sighed happily.

"Huh?" said Persephone. "Nice? Beautiful?"

"But she's frowny and has snake hair!" said Aphrodite.

"Yeah, isn't it great? I like that she's so unusual." Pygmalion gazed at Galatea with love in his eyes. "She's perfect."

"Awww, that's actually kind of sweet," said Aphrodite.

"Yeah, I guess you really do love that paper girl," said Persephone.

"That's what I've been trying to tell you!" said the prince. His eyes narrowed. "Now say a spell to make her come to life. Or else!"

5

Attack!

Aphrodite and Persephone looked at each other, unsure what to do. When they didn't obey him right away, Pygmalion waved his soldiers over. The pink one grabbed Persephone's arm.

"No! Wait! Okay, I'll try to help you if you let my friend go," Aphrodite told the prince. "And if you'll help us find the emerald we came here for."

Pygmalion held up his hand, and his soldiers backed off. "Deal," he replied. "I'll do both, but only if your spell actually works."

Aphrodite gulped. She wasn't all that good at spells yet, but she had to try. "You should probably step away from Galatea," she told him. "In case I bring her to life and she tries to zap you with an eye-ray."

Instead of moving away, though, Pygmalion stepped *closer* to Galatea. He took her hand in his own. "My princess won't hurt me. I'm sure of it."

Aphrodite rolled her eyes.

Hoping for the best, she thought hard to come up with a spell to turn Galatea into a real girl. To her surprise, some magic words just popped into her mind. She stepped closer to Pygmalion and Galatea and spoke them aloud:

"*Give these two a switcheroo.*

So they can share a love that's true.

Make them alike as Pygmalion wishes.

On the count of three magical swishes!"

With that, she swished her arms through the air three times, chanting, "One. Two. *Three!*"

Poof! The two goddess girls leaned forward eagerly. So did the soldiers. Had her spell worked? Had she turned Galatea into a **mortal** like Pygmalion?

"Oh no!" she wailed. It seemed that she *had* made them alike. Both were alive now. But her spell was a boo-boo! "I meant to turn Galatea into a mortal. Instead, I turned Pygmalion into paper!"

"Good job!" shouted Pygmalion. "Galatea *did* come alive. That's what counts."

Huh? Luckily, Pygmalion didn't seem to mind becoming a paper prince. He and Galatea were smiling big at each other! At his signal, the soldiers let Persephone go. She ran over to link arms with Aphrodite.

Aphrodite grinned. "The prince and his new princess look happy!"

"Galatea's smile *is* kind of like Medusa's, though—scary," whispered Persephone.

"When you're in love, I guess you don't notice little stuff like that," Aphrodite said. Making true love happen had filled her with joy!

Before they could remind Pygmalion to help them find the emerald, they heard a loud **whoosh!** The blue soldier ran to look out the window. "A purple dragon snuck into the castle when we weren't looking. It's attacking!" he yelled.

The two girls, the soldiers, and the paper prince and princess ran downstairs and outside. The flying dragon had indeed returned and was now flying around inside the castle walls, still wearing Aphrodite's gold crown, and it was twirling Persephone's silver cane in its claws.

Snort! Its breezy breath and flapping wings sent the paper people swirling high in the air. Pygmalion and Galatea too!

"Help! Stop!" they all shouted. But the dragon didn't stop. ***Snort! Whoosh!***

"Why are you attacking? What do you want?" Aphrodite called to it.

"Oh sure. *Now* you ask," the dragon snorted angrily, circling above the two goddess girls. "I've been trying to give you girls a message. But you ran away!"

"We're sorry! Will you please tell us the message now?" asked Persephone.

"No," the dragon said, pouting. "I'm mad because you've turned Pygmalion into paper!"

Luckily, the dragon stopped whooshing. The paper people floated down to the ground again.

"Why are you mad about that?" Persephone asked it.

"Because I'm lonely. I was going to ask Pygmalion to cut out a paper dragon friend for me. But you've turned him into paper now. So he can't pick up his scissors anymore. They're too heavy for him!"

"We're goddesses," Aphrodite said quickly. "Maybe we can use our magic to find you a friend somehow. If we do, will you return our stuff to us?"

"**Yes!** I'll give you everything! Your crown! Your cane! The jewel!" the dragon blasted.

Aphrodite and Persephone leaned forward in excitement.

"Did you say a jewel?" they asked.

"Yes, that's the message I was trying to tell you," said the dragon. "You're looking for a green emerald, right? The South Wind stole it from Sparkle City. And I stole it from the South Wind!"

"We have to get that emerald!" Persephone whispered to Aphrodite.

Aphrodite nodded. "I have an idea," she called to the dragon. "Even though Pygmalion can't *cut* paper anymore, he can *fold* paper.

Maybe he could make a folded paper dragon friend for you?"

Persephone looked over at Pygmalion. "Could you do that?"

"Sure!" said Pygmalion. "As long as I paint faces on my paper creations, they'll come alive. Folding paper creatures sounds fun. Something new to try. Great idea!"

Looking excited, he hugged Galatea. "Be right back, sweetheart," he told her. He ran into his tower, and she sighed happily, gazing after him.

When he came out again, he was holding a very large piece of orange paper and some paints. Swiftly he folded the paper into a dragon shape. Everyone watched as he painted scales, claws, and wings. Galatea helped him. The minute he finally painted on a face, the folded orange dragon came to life! Its wings fluttered.

The purple dragon floated down to the ground. It snorted at the orange paper dragon. The orange dragon snorted back!

Quickly the purple dragon tossed three objects to the girls. A crown, a silver cane, and a sparkly emerald it had tucked in its feathers! They caught their belongings, and Aphrodite put the jewel in her pocket for safekeeping.

Together the two dragons

lifted off the ground. Then . . . *whoosh!* The happy dragons flew out the castle doors and away, high in the sky. The girls followed and left the castle to the sound of paper-people cheers!

"All is well again in the Kingdom of Cut-Ups," noted Persephone.

"Though they might need to change the castle name to the Kingdom of Fold-Ups!" said Aphrodite. Laughing together, the girls took off along the Hello Brick Road.

6

Friendship

By now the sun was setting, and the sky was turning pink. "It's a long way back to Sparkle City," Aphrodite told Persephone as they hurried away. "It'll be dark before we can get there with the emerald."

Persephone slumped her shoulders. "We'll be too late to save Sparkle City. Maybe we should have asked the purple dragon for a ride."

"Ride? That gives me an idea! I'll call my **chariot**!" said Aphrodite. She clapped her hands together.

Coo! Coo! Suddenly a flock of beautiful white doves pulling a golden chariot appeared overhead. When it zoomed down to the ground, the two girls hopped in.

As they sailed away toward

Sparkle City, Aphrodite heard a tiny voice. "Love is magic," it whispered. The whisper had come from her pocket! *The emerald!* She pulled her pocket open to peek at it. But the jewel spoke no more.

"Did you hear a tiny voice just now?" she asked Persephone.

Persephone shook her head.

"Hmm," said Aphrodite, thinking. "Hey, remember when Hestia told us we were goddesses? I think I might be the goddess of love. Because helping Pygmalion and Galatea find happiness made *me* really happy."

"You could be right! Your love spell worked out great," said Persephone.

Aphrodite smiled. "Thanks! And know what else? I think you might be the goddess of growing things."

Persephone's eyes brightened. "Yes! That sounds perfect. I wonder what Athena and Artemis are the goddesses of?"

Before they could guess, Aphrodite spotted a familiar girl with brown hair. She was walking on the Hello Brick Road far below them. "Look!" she said, pointing.

Persephone looked down. "It's Athena! Let's pick her up!"

Aphrodite guided her chariot downward. As they got closer, Athena saw them and waved. She pulled something small, dark, and round from her pocket. She held it high to show them.

"That must be the black pearl! Athena found it!" Aphrodite said with excitement. "That means we've found three of the jewels! One left to go."

As they flew lower to pick up their friend, Persephone spoke again.

"I hope Artemis is having a great adventure in West Mount Olympus. And that she finds the diamond!"

"Who knows? She may already have it," Aphrodite exclaimed.

As soon as Athena was on board, Aphrodite guided her chariot toward Sparkle City. She hoped they'd spot Artemis soon, because they'd need all four jewels to save the city!

Though the girls weren't yet done with their task, she was happy to be with two of her three best friends. And to have found out what her true magic power was—love! As her doves pulled her chariot higher and higher, Aphrodite's heart soared along with it.

Word List

chariot (CHA•ree•uht): ancient vehicle

diamond (DI•muhnd): A beautiful clear jewel

emerald (EM•er•uhld): A beautiful green jewel

god: A boy or man with magic powers in a Greek myth

goddess (GOD•ess): A girl or woman with magic powers in a Greek myth

Greek myth (mihth): Stories people in Greece made up long ago to explain things they didn't understand about their world

jewels (JULZ): Beautiful costly stones, often made into rings or necklaces

mortal (MOR•tuhl): Human

Mount Olympus (MOWNT oh•LIHM•pus): Tallest mountain in Greece

pearl (PERL): A beautiful jewel found inside an oyster

ruby (ROO•bee): A beautiful red jewel

sparkle (SPAR•kuhl): Shine bright

statue (STA•choo): Carved figure of a person or animal

Questions

1. If you were made out of paper, what might you look like? Can you draw a picture of yourself and some paper friends too?

2. Wind is a problem for the paper people in this book. What other silly or troublesome problems might you have if you were a person, object, or animal made out of paper?

3. Can you make a simple dragon shape by folding a sheet of paper?

4. If you were a god or goddess, what would you want to be the god or goddess of? What magic powers would you want to have?

5. In the next book, Artemis will search for the diamond—the last of the four missing jewels. What adventures do you think she and her goddess-girl friends will have?

Authors' Note

This book is a twist on an ancient **Greek myth** about a mortal artist named Pygmalion. He created a statue of a woman, Galatea. Then Pygmalion fell in love with his statue! This was a problem, because a statue could never love him back. Since Aphrodite was the Greek goddess of love and beauty, he asked her for help. She used her powers to turn his statue into a mortal woman. Pygmalion and Galatea fell in love and lived happily ever after!

—*Joan Holub and Suzanne Williams*